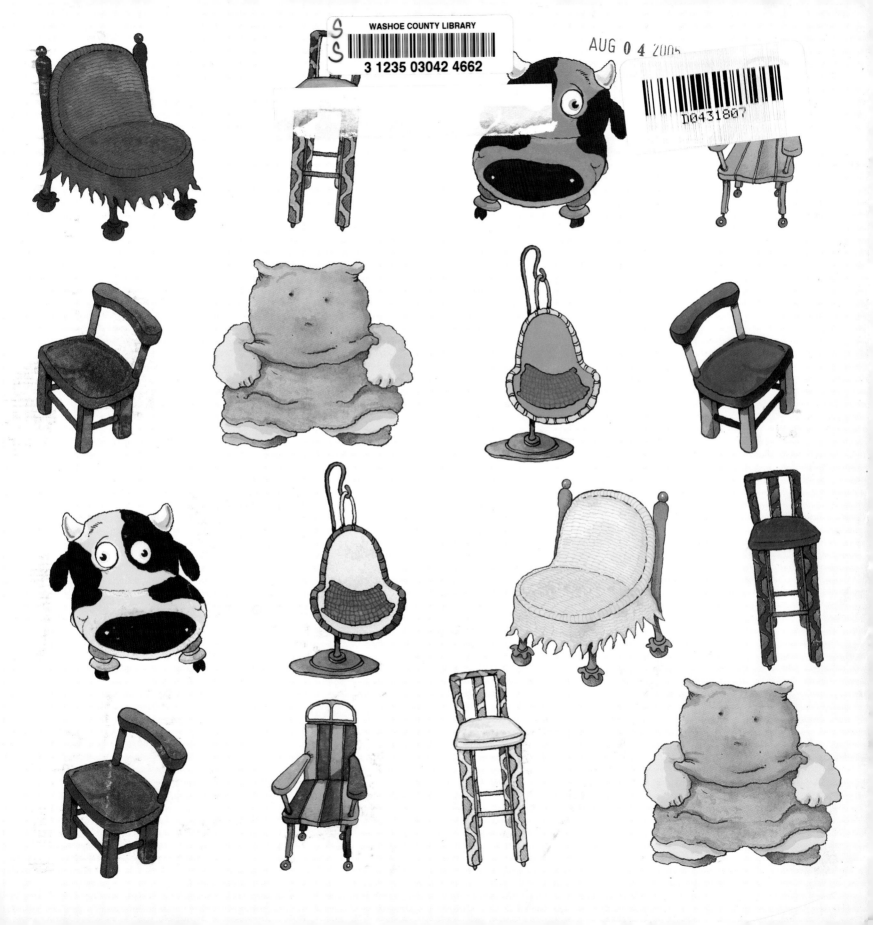

For Vineeta - K. U.

First edition for the United States published
in 2004 by Barron's Educational Series, Inc.

Text copyright © Kaye Umansky 2004
Illustrations copyright © Chris Fisher 2004

The moral rights of the author/artist have been asserted.

First published in the United Kingdom in 2004 by
Oxford University Press
Great Clarendon Street, Oxford OX2 6DP, UK

All inquiries should be addressed to:

Barron's Educational Series, Inc.
250 Wireless Boulevard
Hauppauge, NY 11788
http://www.barronseduc.com

International Standard Book Number 0-7641-5789-2

Library of Congress Catalog Card Number 2004102497

PRINTED IN CHINA
9 8 7 6 5 4 3 2 1

A Chair for Baby Bear

Kaye Umansky Chris Fisher

BARRON'S

"When are you going to fix my chair, Papa?" asked Baby Bear.

"Soon, Baby Bear," said Papa Bear.

"You said that yesterday," said Baby Bear. "And the day before. And the day before that."

"He's right, dear," said Mama Bear. "That naughty Goldilocks broke Baby Bear's chair a very long time ago."

"Well, all right," said Papa Bear.
"I think we'd better look for a
new chair in Bear Town."

"Hooray!" cheered Baby Bear.
"Can we go now?"

The Three Bears set off through the woods. Baby Bear played in the leaves.

"Look at me!" he shouted.
"I'm Robin Hood!"

"Don't get muddy," said Papa Bear.

"Can I have a Robin Hood chair?" begged
Baby Bear. "Please,

please,

please?"

"We'll see," said Mama Bear.

The Three Bears came to a stream.

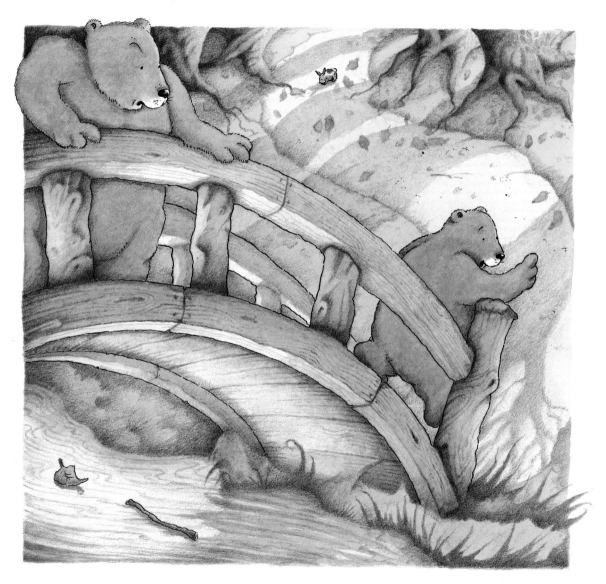

"Look at me!" cried Baby Bear.
"I'm a pirate!"

"Be careful," said Papa Bear. "You'll get wet."

"Can I have a pirate chair?"
begged Baby Bear.

"Please,

please,

please?"

"We'll see," said Mama Bear.

The road wound its way around the hill. In the distance stood a big castle. Baby Bear climbed on a rock.

"I'm the king of the castle!" he shouted.
"Mind you don't fall," said Papa Bear.

"Can I have a king's chair?"
begged Baby Bear.
"Please,
please,
please?"

"We'll see," said Mama Bear.

All the way to Bear Town, Baby Bear thought and thought about the kind of chair he wanted.

When they reached the chair shop, he ran around and around in the revolving doors.

"Stop that at once!" cried Papa Bear. "You'll make yourself sick."

In the shop, there were lots ... and lots ...

and lots ... of chairs.

There was a Robin Hood chair.

But it was much

too scratchy.

There was a Pirate chair.

But it was much

too scary.

There was a King's chair. But it was much too large. The cushion was so big and soft that when Baby Bear sat on it, he sank

down, down, down.

"Don't you like any of them?" asked Mama Bear.

"Ye-e-ss," said Baby Bear.
"But none of them is
quite right."

"Sorry, Baby Bear," said Papa Bear.
"Come on. We'd best be
going home."

Baby Bear was so disappointed. He was tired, too. So Papa Bear gave him a piggyback ride all the way home.

"What's this?" said Mama Bear, as they reached the front door.

There was a big package wrapped in brown paper sitting on the step.

Baby Bear didn't feel tired any more.
He ripped off the paper, opened the box

and. . .

... lifted out the most perfect
Little Red Bear Chair!

With it was a note from Goldilocks.

Dear Baby Bear,

Sorry I broke your chair.

love,
    Goldilocks

Baby Bear tried it out.
"Hooray!" cried Baby Bear.

"It's not too scratchy,

it's not too scary, and it's not too large.

In fact, it's just right."

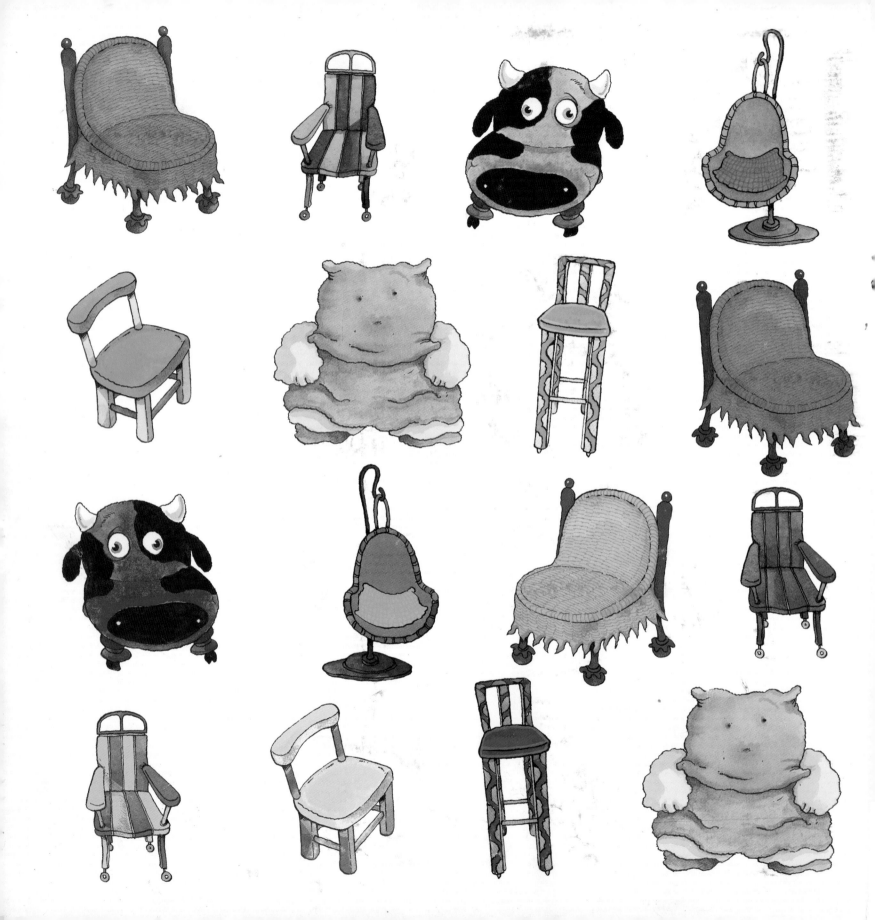